BAD TIMES & GOODBYES

BAD TIMES & GOODBYES

ERMAN M. BARADI

Ermantourage

First Printing, 2023

Dedicated to

Mom, Dad, Erbin, Erson, Rena, Artemis,
Lolo, Lola, Grandma, and Grandpa...

As with everything I do.

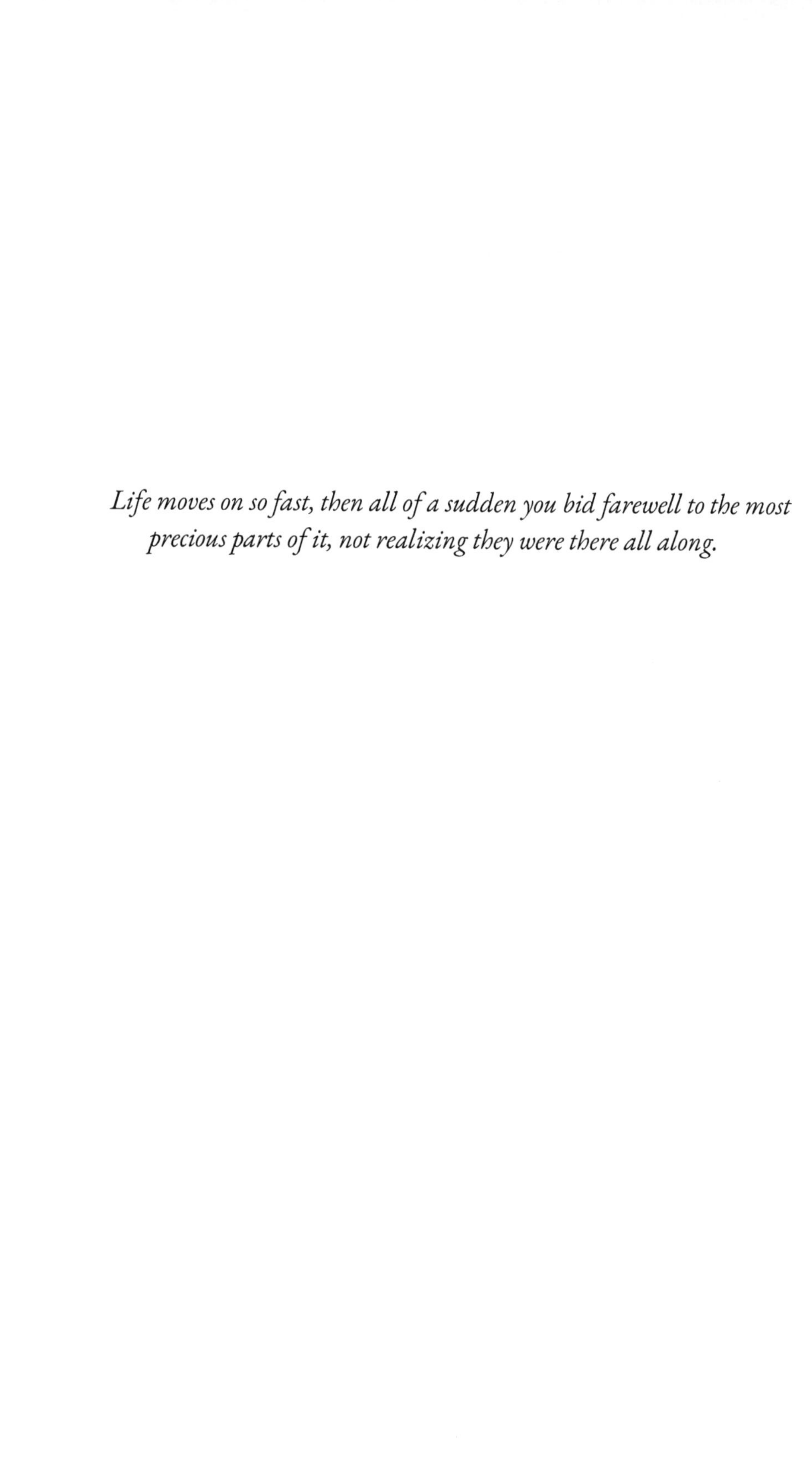

Life moves on so fast, then all of a sudden you bid farewell to the most precious parts of it, not realizing they were there all along.

TABLE OF CONTENTS

"From A Distance"...

"By Choice""...

"The Before/The After"...

"Microphone"...

"Young Holly Would"...

"lonely pLAce"...

"Doctor Said"...

"Sent Me a Storm"...

"Enough Fists"...

"Bullets for Breakfast"...

"Love of Girl/Love of God"...

"Never Broke a Heart"...

"Too Soon"...

"Longing for Drought"...

"At the End of a Dream"...

"Fans"...

"Went to Sleep"...

"Twenty Years Part I"...

"Truly Lived"...

"Goodbye, California"...

"Stop Looking"...

"Day Dream"...

"If Walls Could Talk"...

"Could You Tell Us What It's Like"...

"Lakes and Rain"

"Records"...

"God Gave Us You"...

"A Song to Brother"...

"February Girl"...

"Little Sister"...

"Blue Room"...

"Where the Hero Lives..."

"An Artist"...

"Shore Drive"...

The Promise of Death...

The Greatest

I got them their signings
But I'm barely surviving
Inspiring quote on my feed but I am lying
That feeling inside watching others making their way up
I stay up praying for a miracle to arrive
They think I'm making bank
But I can't even pay for the Uber to the ATM
My parents waiting for that mansion
What do I say to them?
How many times do I tell the world my moment will come?
When I'm seeing some making lump sums
And I'm making none

Life savings? Someone save my life
At this rate I might not make it to May
If I don't prove my independence
It'll be July the latest
I had a vision when I was younger
I called myself the greatest
Ten years go by, what do I have to show for?
My best friend from high school has a Cullinan and a chauffeur
If I hustle this hard, what am I going broke for
It's probably time for a restart
The only thing I can hope for

In a few years I can laugh at what I endured
Crashing on couches, sleeping on floors
Walking down streets with my suitcase
How can I use this pain? 'Cause right now I'm useless
I put my heart in this

There's no stopping this
Something has to give because I thought I found God in this

They think I made it big
I can barely make my bed
No energy to get up and try for the hundredth time again
If the world's a stage, I'm up in the nosebleeds
Clawing my way to the front row seats
Several books that no one's buying
So I didn't bring a pen
No need for signing
I took a look at my first flier
It's been seven years and I'm still just getting by
Where's my million dollar bank account?
I can't pay for an accountant
20,000 followers, but who really counts
When supporters are one percent of the amount
I got so far, but I'm chasing horizons
Seven years and the dream is dying
I thought I'd run the circus but I'm still a clown
Support on the surface but never really turn out

"Moving up in life," they think
But I'm standing still
Trash buried under nice cut grass
I'm a landfill
Parents calling me home
"Are these your plans still?"
Captain of a sinking boat and
Filling all the holes that I can fill

I need a big break but I'm breaking big
I committed to the dream and this beer keg
Drinking my body to death

Waiting for the dream, is it here yet?
Looks like my paycheck and my fears met
Seven years later I sit in silence
No one should know what's on my mind
Looking back at all my time spent
2020 killed my momentum and I fell behind
Now they won't buy tickets but will come for free
Or not show up though they RSVP'd
2023 they're all on strike
I'm not writing movies but I'm writing lines

They think I'm doing fine
I'm barely surviving
The quote on my feed can never describe it
That feeling inside watching others making their way up
I stay up praying for a miracle to arrive
But after seven years I cannot escape it
Point of no return despite the points of breaking
So what's the point in waiting
I've been hitting pavement
One day I'll stand on stages
And know I made it
The greatest

Christmas Trees

Took the last flight home
To save some dollar bills
Layover in a new town
To catch new thrills
The longer I hold out
To see mom and dad
The longer I wait
To see what I once had
I touch down on familiar ground
But where did the familiar go?
I come home and I freeze
Christmas trees don't feel like they used to
They're shorter than I recall
And I'm not even that tall
Take a look at these streets
They're a bit thinner than I'm used to
I was just here last fall
But it's like I never lived here at all
I come home and I freeze
The older I get, the greener the grass
But the browner the leaves
Who took over my favorite bar?
They dropped my favorite beer
Did they repaint my seat
Or is it a brand new chair?
The city has the same name
But not the same feel
I come home and I freeze
Christmas trees don't feel like they used to
They're shorter than I recall
And I'm not even that tall

Take a look at these streets
They're a bit thinner than I'm used to
I was just here last fall
But it's like I never lived here at all
Took the last flight out
When I had to leave
The greener the grass
But the browner the leaves

Cold Waters: Part I

A long day at work
He has nothing left to give
Can barely keep his eyes open
On the ride back home
When he spots a woman
About to jump off the bridge
Can barely keep her eyes open
Four hundred feet from the water below
Approaches her slowly
"There's a lot of life to live"
Walks up with arms open
To talk her off the edge
They both stand there in silence
Eyes swelling with tears, they couldn't hide them
Got up on the ledge and sat beside her
"If you jump you're not jumping alone"
She couldn't fathom a stranger falling into cold ocean
Knowing it was all to stop her from deciding
To jump when there's a lot of life to live
Maybe there's a reason for these two to collide
He guides her back to the sidewalk
They sit against the wall for a few minutes to talk
He swears she's seen her before somewhere
They begin to chat about how they've both swim colder waters
Skeletons in their closets, a bit too honest
She just got out of prison, fifteen years for a car wreck
Then it finally hits him
She was the drunk driver who took one of his daughters...

Life of Luxury

She's glued to the gram
Scrolling through feeds that don't
Make her feel any better
Hot bodies on yachts in warmer weather
Is it selling the boat or selling the city?

She's on this side of the screen
So she doesn't feel pretty
She asked what could set her free
I said, "You're too in love with the luxury
Life is good when you let it be
Comparison kills, and you're a casualty"

We can spend our lives window shopping
Long for designer shades fit for island hopping
Nothing wrong with catching flights
But there's still life behind your current curtains
She's scrolling down the feed
Somehow they're in Ibiza and Rio
In the same week
Where does she live and how many mouths to feed?
I said

You can be the best swimmer but lose your friend to the sea
Love people, not luxury
Not a jab at billion dollar companies
They also have tables to fill
But don't get addicted to chasing the scene
As much as your prescription pills

Some of us look for soulmates

In those without souls
Disappointed we use the right people
For the wrong roles
You can travel half the world
But there's no feeling like home
Save up your pennies to be like them
But there's so much for free
Love yourself before luxury

Best Picture

Sadly saw this coming
Thought you'd be my someone
Till the day you took off running from me
Sometimes what wins Best Picture
Is still the saddest fiction
And we did better than nominees

I played this story in my head
I kept the middle and changed the end
Not what I intended, but
The reason why you love me is the reason why I let you down
The perfect picture's faded at the edges
Same movie, two cuts of the edit

The locks are the same but I can't get in
Is there something I'm forgetting?
Or does home not feel warm anymore
Our dinner's not perfectly plated
Like they were when we first dated
Since when does homefront feel like war?
Can we go back to the middle?
Right before the story fizzled

I played this story in my head
I kept the middle and changed the end
Not what I intended, but
The reason why you love me is the reason why I let you down
The perfect picture's faded at the edges
Same movie, two cuts of the edit

Hi there, it's nice to meet you

I don't know what you have been through
But I'd love to know you over time
I caught your smile across the party
Recovered from broken hearted
You've got your scars and I've got mine

Hi again, it's nice to see you
Let's see where this'll lead to
I'm scared to open up again
Love's never perfectly shaped
Unlike our dinner plates
But I like how this begins

I played this story in my head
I kept the middle and changed the end
Not what I intended, but
The reason why you love me is the reason why I let you down
The perfect picture's faded at the edges
Same movie, two cuts of the edit

Half Time

God is first in your lineup
That's completely fine
He's first in mine too
Except on the bad nights
When I forget I need Christ

Did you think about next week
Deciding on what you're planning
Is it weighing on your mind
Too heavy for standing
At least you made it so far, thank Christ

We're at half time
Of an already short life
Did you catch that flight?
Dance to your favorite record all night?
Make the most of a short time

Isn't it crazy
Pulling at sunflowers to pushing up daisies
But you still have days to unwind
Standing at half time
Your face has changes
But you're no stranger
Silver linings playbook
We're just all on different pages

Don't be afraid of the marks on your skin
They're like maps of where you've been

Don’t count the candles, count the blessings
You’re younger than the years we’re in

We’re at half time
Of an already short life
Did you catch that flight?
Dance to your favorite record all night?
Make the most of a short time

Isn’t it crazy
Pulling at sunflowers to pushing up daisies
But you still have days to unwind
Standing at half time

Attic

They say the friendzone doesn't exist
But I kept persisting
Insisted I was the perfect fit
I'm not talking wedding rings
Or making you my misses
Just saying I'd give you everything in this instant
Go on dates and talk about our interests
Talk about the future over drinks and five star dishes
But you had your eye on someone else
Who kept asking for forgiveness
You don't see me like I see you
Sometimes I'm invisible
But that's okay because only you can choose your happiness
So if it's him you want I'm rooting for that bliss
But I see something that you've missed
Maybe you sensed it too but "happy" had you hesitant
Rain or shine, around here it started trickling
Pain and love, looks like he couldn't tell the difference
If I'm being honest, he's a prick
I found her in the attic
A needle in her veins
What did he do to you?
What did he put you through?
I found her in the attic
Nothing was left the same
She was hoping for something better
But she was accustomed to the pain
It was the weekend and I tried to rein her in
It was no longer romance
I just wanna save a friend
She gave him another chance

But that's addiction, isn't it?
Inches away from death but you're still itching for it
Too blinded to see others because he was hovering
They weren't arms to cover you but to smother you
Black and blue, bruised up, now recovering
Out of the hospital and right back to him
But that's addiction, isn't it?
At first I tried to win you over
But I just wanna see you survive the night
We can talk about "us" another time
But maybe there's no time for later
What will it take to save her?
A mixture of intervention and Jesus Christ?
In his parked car again
Neighbors hear the arguing
What is about this dude you keep running back to
But you're just running laps around the sun
Getting burned at every touch
I've almost given up
And then...
I found her in the attic
A needle in her veins
What did he do to you?
What have they put you through?
I found her in the attic
Nothing was left the same
She was hoping for something better
But she was accustomed to the pain
Now you're two months over him
It says so on your chip
You found your step
And you haven't rebound or found someone worse than him
And I see that you're glowing too
I'm two months over you

Sorry if that's not what you want to hear
But you had one too many shots
No longer in the attic for you
But you're not in the attic too

Future Child

May you see the world through your mama's eyes
You'll be bad some days, you'll be wild
But you'll be mine
My future child

Turn me into a man on a different level
You'll drive me mad some nights, you'll be a rebel
But you'll be mine
My future child

If you ever see me cry, know that I tried
And I'll wear that smile for you
My future --

They'll tell you what to believe
You don't have to agree
But be kind
You're bound to fall to peer pressure
But it won't be forever
Hold your ground
I won't crack the code to fatherhood
But may it always feel this good
My future child

You'll get hurt sometimes
And that's fine
You'll shake it off with just a little time
Bruises come easy
Healing comes hard
Living through it makes up who you are
No makeup to cover up your battle scars

I won't be perfect
But I'm perfectly yours

Your future father
Give you more than my eyes
Be there for as long as I'm alive
My future child

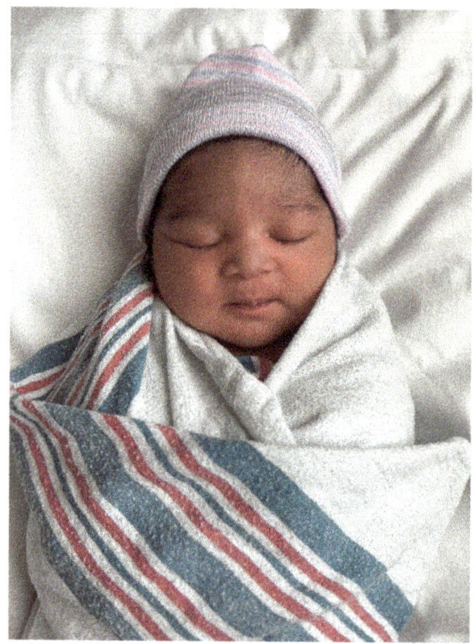

My niece, Artemis

Photo by Hughes Le

Picket Fences

Heard a song on the radio I could've wrote better
Watched a movie on the telly I could've wrote
Pretty girls out there who'd never open my love letters
Maybe someday I can flex the logo on my coat
Catch up with kids from graduation
Teachers said they're going places
I see them with children and white picket fences
In my defense, I chose rhyming words
In hopes the world would listen
I am still learning even after my degree
They told me, oh, the possibilities when you're twenty-three
Finding others who find their strides
Did I just not wake up in time?
I'm just gonna say it
Hurry up and make me famous
So I can put my folks on vacation
Siblings can retire at early ages
Not retire to early graves
Because the pennies in their pockets
Don't match up to what they gave
What's tomorrow's date?
I have some choices to make?
Some history to save
After all the mistakes I create
Not trying to be famous
Just put my parents in a mansion
And live off of savings
Look at my life and
Say that I made it
Retire my siblings
And make all the payments
Take a road less traveled

Lay the concrete and pave it
All the while try my best
To keep the faith up
But times get delayed
On our next adventure
I want to take flight
But we're gravity centered
Everyone trying be famous
I just wanna my fly my family
To nicer places
Put them up in their dream mansion
Flip the sign to "no longer vacant"
Swipe the card in Vegas without
Checking what's in the bank account
And know we made it
I'm just gonna say it
Baptized in a pool and I can't swim
Maybe that's the point of it
Having faith that I'll be saved from drowning
Turn that frown downside up
Lord willing, fill my cup
I'm a little parched when there's water all around me
I'll ask the neighbors what they think
Breezing by on their porch swings
"Is the grass truly greener
Because you have a yard?"
They said don't think they don't have it hard
A mix grit and luck from the one in charge
While I'm standing with a suitcase
That's taped together in several different parts
Heard a song on the radio I could've wrote better
Watched a movie on the telly I could've wrote
At least I have the chance for greener pastures
And not trapped on the smaller side of the moat

...gives meaning to life...

Three

The number of years I faced the truth
You booked a one way ticket
But I'll walk to the terminal with you
Tell me what you need to hear
As long as it lessens your fears
Board the plane, we'll take it from here
What should I say?

I pray you peace at the terminal
Don't be afraid of your next flight
Wipe your tears and don't call it goodbye
Someday I'll take the trip too
But for now I'll walk to the terminal with you

Two
The hours till I have to leave
I didn't wish you'd get home this soon
Remember how you'd count me down from three
And all the monsters left the room?
Short term passengers in a long term place
Close your eyes, let the light fill the space
You've lived your years and dealt with the pain
It's selfish of me to beg you to stay
What should I say?

I pray you peace at the terminal
Don't be afraid of your next flight
Wipe your tears and don't call it goodbye
Someday I'll take the trip too
But for now I'll walk to the terminal with you

This won't be the last time
So no need for last words
Except "I love you" and "I always will"
Hold your ticket, they're calling the line
You can leave your luggage behind
It's fine, we'll take it from here...

One...
Don't be afraid of your next flight
Wipe your tears and don't call it goodbye

Perfect for Me

There they go again
Running for the hills
Like penguins to the ocean
Without a sense of chill
Could I be the issue?
No way that I'm that bad

It's by accident but I'm out here playing victim
I thought I was adequate just by simply existing
I try to get it out, it's balled up in my system
A better version of me inside dying to persist
Could I be the issue?
No way that I'm that bad

Make no mistake, I didn't think I could make them
Until ten broken friendships and saw I'm the problem
Something about my ego figured I walked on perfectly
I guess I'm the only one perfect for me

There I go again
Running at the mouth
Always up on my high horse
Without a sense of south
Could I be the issue?
No way that I'm that bad

It's by accident but I'm evil in transition
Of finding if the good in me could possibly exist
I try to get it out, it's somewhere in my system
A better version of me inside lying to persist

And I guess it's not the people all around me that are defensive
Please come back, I could use a laugh at someone else's expense
And I left my wallet at home
Perhaps this is the norm
One half of me is tired playing victim
One half of me isn't familiar with his system
One whole of me would like to trade places...

Make no mistake, I didn't think I could make them
Until ten broken friendships and saw I'm the problem
Something about my ego figured I walked on perfectly
I guess I'm the only one perfect for me

Morning Bell

Dear Davy
I thought of you today
May you have what you sought years before
May the sound of a bell not bring you grief
I see you're doing fine now
Found the woman of your dreams

High school wasn't the easiest on you
Yet high school isn't the society it seems
But you found your one and you've got your house
Making your mother and daddy proud
A career that suits you just right
That you've never imagined
Getting pushed around the lunch line

Dear Davy
Crazy to think it's so much better now
And everyone's changed I bet
They'd say sorry if you let them
Ask to start over if you met them
No need to hide on Friday nights
You're welcome into any event you'd like
Mom and dad dropping you off is a precious thing
Moments we hold onto nowadays
When the morning begins you're not afraid
A whole day to look forward to
Not run from
Honest to God, glad you stuck around
Made your way to being somebody's someone

Dear Davy
Thought of you today
As an old face wished me well
Thought of you even if I was among the ones
Who made you fear the morning bell

Art by Rubin Baradi

Come to Me

I'm no saint
Never claim to be
But when you have issues you lay them on me
And I listen
But I insist
I'm just another addicted to the bottle
Drinking hard to forget

Remember when you'd go, with every heartbreak you'd come across?
Overtime you slowed down, you felt nothing serviced you
Thought a mass of people couldn't imagine what you've gone through
We all fall prey to devils disguised as truth

Reaching that point where you've got no return
Don't see your miles ahead of where you've come from
You're looking for something
Listening to whoever preaches
If you don't come to me, I understand
But come to Jesus

Struggling with faith
You seek salvation in pretty faces on Saturdays
But make no mistake
It doesn't have to be that way

Running to me like I've got an answer or two
When I'm over here with the same questions as you

Remember when we'd go, with every heartbreak we'd come across?
Overtime we slowed down, we felt nothing serviced us

Thought a mass of people couldn't imagine what we've gone through
We all fall prey to devils disguised as the truth

Reaching that point where you've got no return
Don't see your miles ahead of where you've come from
You're looking for something
Listening to whoever preaches
If you don't come to me, I understand
But come to Jesus

Clawing and crawling but you're falling for easy
I can go with you because I also need this
Reaching that point where you've got no return
Don't see your miles ahead of where you've come from

You're looking for something
Listening to whoever preaches
If you don't come to me, I understand
But come to Jesus

Photo by Electric Victory

Pretty Enough to Make My Own Cover

Shift Alt Delete on my last few minutes
My body was involved but my mind wasn't in it
Run it back for me before the media spins it
But wait, I'm not famous yet
Do I want the security or do I not
Have to watch my back every second
Do you want financial security or not?
At the price of getting recorded every second

I'm a man, I can cry
And they'll call it weak
But if I don't, they say it's toxicity
Throw their harsh words at patriarchy
Lead more or lead less?
Exactly what do they want from me?

Speak up for what's right
As long as it's written by the left
Sponsors and reps
Handlers and publicists

They said I have talent
Took me years to find it
The world ain't so pretty with opinions
Maybe I took years to hide it
Want the world to see your words?
Sign here, contractually binding
Now endorse this candidate
And follow him blindly

Do I have to be as single as my song on the radio?

They asked, "How much do you want to be famous though?"
We'll sponsor the bottles
Go to the club and find the hottest supermodel
Give us a story to tell in the morning
But what if I want a wife and kids?
I'm a traditionalist
Suits and ties carry a big stick
"Follow suit, we gave you these views"
Beachfront, Youtube, and politics

Sit down, shut up
You're only pretty enough to make your own cover
Only say what's on the pages
Or we'll go out there and find another
They made the Devil Wear Prada
Then mailed her a hundred products
To post about on Instagram
And review all the options

Is this really what I came here for?
To give my parents the life they prayed for
The doctor's bill taken care of
At the price of my mental wealth
Can I ever get out of bed
Without someone wanting me dead
Another lawsuit, months wasted in a courtroom
A slip and fall in my living area
By someone who called me a friend

Sit down, shut up
You're only pretty enough to make your own cover
If you wish for more than fifteen minutes
Don't be so stubborn

No need for finding someone
We assigned you a lover

Sit down, chin up
We need another headshot
Next time you fall out of line
You're back to a desk job
The movie is crap but I'll lie to your face
My name's on the poster
No wonder "fortune" sounds a bit like "torture"
They told me it'd hurt my credibility
But at least I get exposure
Be like your rich friends and afford the chauffeur
Vocal cords are shot, but they want another song
So keep on singing this sing along

Control Alt Delete on my life decisions
Before they write my check for the sixteenth minute

Celebrity Snow Angel

She's top of the bill, top of the charts
She can do anything and they'll call it art
Started from the bottom and she's gotten this far
Celebrity snow angel, she's just playing her part
Throw on the wings
If they want they'll clipped them
The ones who call the shots
Stuck a needle in her
Coached by socialite
Makes her feel she really needs him
Truth be told there's a demon in him

Middle of summer but she's covered in snow
Sponsored by Pepsi but clearly loves coke
Two hours late to the next show
Got us all speculating
Chasing the dollar led to chasing the devil
She's playing the game and reached another level
A Hulu documentary and a Netflix special
Placements on streamers, she's truly Amazin

Celebrity preacher on speed dial
Doesn't recognize her voice, it's been a while
She's playing the game and reached another level
We've all got demons but she found several
She's top of the bill, top of the charts
She can do anything and hear their applause
Hitting the bottom and everybody nose
Celebrity sponsored by Pepsi
But clearly loves Coke
Another celebrity angel found laying in snow

Strengthen The Heart

I looked my whole life for Eden
Been seeking greener grasses
I didn't stand where I needed
So I made home in other pastures
Took some time to realize
It's not the garden that needs more water
You can build a fountain where you want it
And the food won't ever harvest
I want to strengthen the heart
And narrow my path
Lead it to you, closer to you
Teach me to strengthen my heart
Because my roots are damaged
I couldn't choose where I'm planted
But still wish to be closer to you
It can take a whole life to find Eden
But it's just going back to where I started
Move me, or move through me so others believe it
And leave room to change the brokenhearted
Took some time to realize
It's not the garden that needs me finding
I can be anywhere and there's a reminder
There are no grapes without the vine
I want to strengthen the heart
And narrow my path
Lead it to you, closer to you
Teach me to strengthen my heart
Because my roots are damaged
I couldn't choose where I'm planted
But still wish to be closer to you

I Just Want You

Our beginning was like anyone else's
Chasing you after a shooting a shot or two
But you let me in after coming to your senses
All I needed was the taste of you
Everything going right until you saw a change
I started acting funny when the money came
Sat me down right before breakfast
Said it's best we call it now before we both break

Packed your things and called a cab
Because no one's good spirits could lyft you up
Told me my career was the only thing I wanted bad
"I can show you proof, I just want you"
And you still walked out and didn't look back

Our beginning was like anyone else's
Chasing you with a shot or two
Getting over her and drinking you
All I needed was a case of you
Forgot what I had to forgive her for
The drunken nights are what I liver for
Slipped you in right before breakfast
Then the doctor said just another sip is reckless

Packed my things and called the cab
Snuck wines and spirits into some cups
Made a last call as we got to rehab
This 100 proof, I just want you
But I dumped you out and never looked back

Our beginning was like anyone else's
Chasing me as I run away from you
It was at my lowest that I came to my senses
Pray for healing and ask for forgiveness
Everything going wrong until I had to change
Someone taught me "you shall call his name"
Said a little blessing right before breakfast
Took a second to slip You onto my necklace

Packed my things and called the cab
The spirit of Jesus and an overflowing cup
Didn't meet me at my best but where I'm at
"I have enough proof, I just want You"
Goodbye to my past life and I never looked back

Ain't the City

LA ain't the city I first loved
The magic left after a summer like my first love
The city's what you make it
With the right paycheck
Or maybe there's a bigger fight I could've put up

Or maybe I should've gone sooner
At some point the sun sets on honeymooners
Then reality settles in
I'm a heartbreak veteran
Maybe it's the right city and I'm the wrong suitor

LA ain't the city I first loved

The Oscars make it look like the walk
Of fame is on pristine blocks
But after the stars it's hard to breathe
The smell of piss, weed, and failed dreams
Anyway I miss the red and yellow of leaves

LA ain't the city I first loved

I fell to the system to try and fit in
But I woke up and got tired of playing victim
I dropped fifty bucks on a taco truck
Dropped my day to hit the gym to try and look fit
But I woke up to my bed two feet from the kitchen
They said stay away and I decided not to listen

Everybody's on drugs, am I missing out?
Chasing cash cows, they're chasing clout

Can we tell the difference
Between recreation and prescription?
Are we seeking love or seeking views?
Do you wish to see the world
Or for the world to see you?

LA ain't the city I first loved

I fell to the system to try and fit in
But I woke up and got tired of playing victim
I dropped fifty bucks on a taco truck
Dropped my day to hit the gym to try and look fit
But I woke up to my bed two feet from the kitchen
They said stay away and I decided not to listen

I'll be back again and learn to love you better
I'll be back again if you love me better
Don't need a new prescription
Just need someone to listen
LA ain't the city I first loved
I fell to the system to try and fit in
But I woke up and got tired of playing victim
I dropped fifty bucks on a taco truck
Dropped my day to hit the gym to try and look fit
But I woke up to my bed two feet from the kitchen
They said stay away and I decided not to listen

Dive Bar

She sips slow on her red wine
Tells herself it's the final time
"Who's gonna come save me tonight?"
She lives her life in disarray
All these days just feel the same
"Is it my third or thirteenth bottle today?"

Watching her from across the terrace
A dress that says "I want to meet someone"
Or a dress that says "I am someone"
A face that says she wants to be someone else
Her waitress paints on a smile
Just enough tips to make it home 50 miles
Half her check to fix her tires
All so she can come here and wear out her smile
She has a baby to feed on her own
Not enough walls to make up a home
Paint chipping, faucet won't stop dripping
Customers poorly tip
As she stands there painting her smile

Yelled at by a manager who's physically there
But whose mind is consumed by a sister
who's about to check out
The treatment's stop working and
she's losing her hair
The manager's ready to burst into tears
and head out
But he can't let his staff see him
break in a business setting
Every little thing triggers and upsets him

It's a slow evening and nothing's going right
Praying God will grant his sister another night

Takes it out on a waitress who
just dropped another bottle
Who wishes she wasn't there but
has no other options
Losing hope in the savings she's been
adding by the pile
Sweeping up the broken glass
as she fakes another smile

She swings by the lounge singer who hates his guitar
Six strings that promised he'd make it much further
An audience that barely whispers his name
Full on drunk and drowning out his voice
But it's a gig that pays rent this month
Enough to get by on cigarettes and lunch
An audience that barely realizes his shame
As he reflects on what became of his last life choice

He sings to a crowd of under ten
One of whom sips her wine
Wondering why she's back there again
Maybe he's the one who'll save her tonight

Two Cents

There was life in you
I wanted to protect him
But you made a decision before I put my two cents in
As a man, and you said I have no stake in this
And you announced it to the world like it's breaking news
Did it for the likes, did it for the views
Meanwhile my heart's breaking
I lost both my child and my muse
Packed my suitcase and for some reason it left you confused
Told me thinking I had any rights was misconstrued
Didn't even get an even conversation
Said history is on your side
Why does it feel like nobody's on mine?

There was life in you
I wanted to protect him
I'm a man, and you said it didn't matter my perspective
Doctor sat me down gently
Told me from now on I'm shooting blanks
Apparently, I'm running on empty
And only had this one chance
A storm raged in me
Mercy, reign over me
Because there's no future in us
And there'll never be another me
Took a step outside the office
Broke down crying in the waiting room
The whole line at the reception staring holes
Didn't feel like a man anymore
The world thinks it's just a one time thing
And I'll have plenty more options

Stomach nauseous
How can I walk back into the doctor's office?
Spent two years chasing you, rejection come rejection
Finally got the ball, but didn't get the tether
A blessing or a lesson?
Guess it comes down to perspective

There was life in you
And I wanted to protect him
Hit the bottle hard
Asking God for a bargain
She is somebody's daughter
Did she think of other options?
I've downed all the vodka
Two more drops from the bottom
Heard a heartbeat in March
Wanted to be a father come autumn
They're all laughing at my tears
Said history is on your side
Why does it feel like nobody's on mine?

There was life in you
And I wanted to protect him
Could barely say a few words
Before the world objected

Death of Sadness

What is pain but a four letter word
Equal to love and drug
But it comes for free
I tried to milk this out
To last a long time
But then one day the feeling left me

What's this newness?
Something like empty
I paid for the drug
But someone who offered love was tempting
Death to regrets
There's only one life to live
But who's counting
I'm no good at math
Death to bitterness

Some would think it never ends
So take this hurt that latched on
And the air can have it back
You're a person, not a punching bag
I won't use you to absorb my past

Curated the pages
But you can't cure me
Books sell me on a better me
From worn out to worthy
But what is heal but a four letter word
I suppose we should put more effort
Into making love a verb
And it'll come free

Death to regrets
There's only one end to get
And may it be when we most expect
May the next six pack hit different
Celebration with loved ones and friends
Now that's the one life to live

Death to sadness
Once the madness sets in
And we see their way out
Without the return of regretting

Growing up has its comedowns...

Venetian Starbucks

Working early at the register
Too damn early to work
6am, it's Tuesday again

Third person already to bitch about the cold brew
Not sweet enough, not bitter enough
Too damn early to clock in

We're all staring every minutes at our watches
Stay home and make your own Folgers
Another minute, another day of getting older
How am I going to save the world
From this side of the counter?

Got visions bigger than this Malibu Dream
Losing it; not even the same company
Regardless, watching the minutes till five hits

Throw on my cape and save this city
I have the power in me
Watch me fly
Right over this Venetian luxury
City of Sin needs some saving
And Jesus takes his break at the slot machine

If only they knew I can lift grown men above my shoulders
Spin them before I toss them down
Maybe they'd place their bets on me
Instead of asking for their coffee black and their sugar brown

I can save corner shops from burglaries

And retrieve cats from burning trees
The mayor would award me with a key
But I'm just serving him coffee black and sugar brown

Opened early to work the register
Too damn early to work
6am, it's Wednesday again

Excalibur

Janitor at Excalibur
Her red glasses match her work outfit
And bashful attitude
Tosses ashes into a trash can
For twelve bucks an hour
Surrounded by winners with six figures
Her life isn't figured out yet
Dumping ash trays into trash cans
Too busy to light her own cigarette
Running this hamster wheel amidst the rat race
Cleaning all day to keep her mind out of a bad place
Got a part-time being a busker outside of Luxor
Tried to count her blessings to keep the demons at bay
Been six years since she lost her best friend
Next door at the Mandalay

Takes the bus back home to Henderson
A ride long enough to think of better days
Gets back to her dusty apartment and seven cats
Looks at a life that could've been
Rocking all red but should've bet on black
Warms up her leftovers
Been years since a man's been over
Tears hit her kitchen counter
No one sticks around any longer
Thinks of a life that could've been

Nightfall comes she hits the bridge
Grabs her strings and starts singing
A few covers from someone more famous
Quarters flung into her guitar case

See what joy she brings
Catches the smiles of passersby as she sings the bridge
When a gentle soul catches her eye
The crowd hangs for ten seconds then go on
But he sticks around a little longer
Says he's in town for just a few
But visits every month or two
He'd love to hear her sing again
If he can ask for custom requests
He stayed through twenty more songs

"Come sunrise I'll be gone"
She performed for him on an empty corner
Not knowing if it'll be their last time
Now singing wasn't just a pastime
Played the classics for him
Hit every note like it's her lifeline
She knew the sun would come up any time
Said he'd see her when he's back in town
But he has business and dogs to tend to for now
Exchanged numbers and final glances
And like a vampire he vanished with the sun

She threw on her reds and downed some morning meds
After coffee, put on her bashful attitude
Tosses ashes into a trash can
And it's barely 6 a.m.
Surrounded by winners with six figures
Her life isn't figured out yet
Dumping ash trays into trash cans
But with the confidence to light her own cigarette

Rio

He booked a suite in Vegas on a Monday
Overlooks the strip for the photo ops
$26 a night at Rio
Wishing he could afford Brazil'
He came here to be a performer
Strip off his clothes for photo ops
Hopes of $2000 a night in tips
Maybe he can live that dream still

And maybe he'd fall in love in Paris
Wishing he could be in France
Dance under the lights of Fremont
And dream he still had a chance
Of sweating under spotlights
And meeting a sweet face in the crowd
Scraping by on $26 a room a night
At least he is for now

Old enough to make it on his own
Young enough to grit his teeth and
not break his bones
Just enough skill to merit a microphone
It's the age to make the stage his home
Maybe he'll find romance at Venetian
Pretend like they're in Venice
Have the world in his palms
Quit his day job and not regret it

Raise his kids in Summerlin
Millions earned from all the shows

And as soon as winter begins
Another year of performances to go

But here he is in Rio
Looking at the world below
From his 29th floor window
Wishing he could afford São Paulo
But how long can he last in Vegas?
Seeing all the A-list who actually made it
The lights stay on but his dreams have faded
Is it all a mirage of what fame is?

He booked a suite in Vegas on a Friday
Can invest in the views but not in photoshop
He upgraded to the weekend rates
To see what Saturday offered
Maybe busk for visitors at the corner shop
And be discovered by some promotion
Maybe his family will see that he's devoted
And finally quit from trying to stop him
Maybe he'll find his way to MGM
A million singers wish they could be him
Wouldn't resemble what he used to be
Not in the vaguest

Started from Rio and reached the Strip
Making more than the average tip
Started from outside the scene
And now he feels he's made it
For now he'll dream from Rio
Okay not being in Brazil
Because he's got a city to conquer
As long as he stays he will

Art by Rubin Baradi

Never Too Late

She believed all her life
Just couldn't get her husband to follow suit
Years of trying to get him to church
Were years of him not following through
How could he live in a world like this
And think miracles exist
Then came the news
His heart won't last another attack
Best to keep him comfortable
He stared his wife in the face and asked aloud
"Who is this man you speak of?
I could use him right now."

After 85 years he gave his life to Jesus
One month later he would leave us
It's never too late to find freedom
Never too late to find freedom

She lived her entire youth
Staring straight into the mirror
No matter the diets she put herself through
The model on TV could never be her
How could she live in a world like this
And think everyone gets happiness
Then came the day
Left a note behind for her roommate to find
Then went on her way
She stared at her doctor who pumped out the pills
"Is there someone I can listen to?
This time I will."

After three attempts she gave her life to Jesus
Just another minute she wouldn't be here
It's never too late to reach them
Never too late to reach them

He lived half his life
Sitting on 25-to-life
The things he's seen on the inside
Enough to make a preacher cry
How could he live in a world like this
And think we get second chances
Then came the news
He's getting off sooner the Sunday after next
A second chance he better use
He stared his cellmate in the eye and said
"The book you've been reading,
I think I need it."

After prison he gave his life to Jesus
It took this long to see it
It's never too late to redeem them
Never too late to redeem them

Wynwood

Traded a suitcase for spray paint
She feels at home hovering over pavement
Basketball courts and Wynwood Walls
She didn't care for commission
Not like what she needed in California to survive
She did it for the love of mixing neon pinks with turquoise
Realism with escapism
Escaping the standard 9-to-5
Getting by on donations
She went viral for making a statement on
Modern day technology enslavement
Among other artists
But alone in her own world
Her own block of concrete
Her own section of wall
This is her calling
Maybe she'll never afford the penthouse
But whoever does will pay her to paint it

Funny Like That

Busy living, busy for a buck
Is it from the hustle or is it from the luck?
Finally made your first million
When the drunk driver struck
Life's funny like that
Wishing for things you didn't have
Just to miss the people you never lacked
You spend your life wearing helmets
Just to get stabbed in the back
Yeah, life's funny like that

Don't let anger be a hang up
Years are too short to act like strangers
If we're bound for heaven anyway
What's the point of little things getting in our way?
The good die young
The bad die good
It's those final seconds they'd take back the evil
If they could

Staying stuck on the betrayal won't give you freedom
We can hate Judas but Judas was needed
Life's too short, don't make it shorter
Wasting time in the dark hiding underneath the covers
You've got a beauty you shouldn't hide
Even losers win over lovers
Remember that time you didn't pass the quiz
And you thought that was the end of it
All this time later it doesn't mean a thing
Life's funny like that

A few bruises and welts on skin
Several attempts to find their way in
They can't kill if you won't let them
Don't you prefer it like that
Don't let anger be a hang up
Years are too short to act like strangers
If we're bound for heaven anyway
What's the point of little things getting in our way?

Stories Do

First impressions don't always hit this hard
When you'd see my face you didn't always see stars
You shared your drink with others and never felt love
Finally gave me a sip and now here we are
Something to tell our mothers
When they meet each other
The last you choose is technically the last in line
Sun hits our faces on the summer drive
Can we feel like this for a long, long time?
Store this memory and bask with you
Summers don't last forever but stories do
As the city slumbers I'll dance with you

Every season has "we're closed" signs
Lord knows we can't drink all the time
You turned over a new leaf and it made you fall
For the first good guy to come along
Something to tell our brothers
When they meet each other
The lasting choice is technically the last you find
You couldn't see me at the starting line
Sun hits our faces on the summer drive
Can we feel like this for a long, long time?
Store this memory and bask with you
Summers don't last forever but stories do
As the city slumbers I'll dance with you

Art by Rubin Baradi

Immortal Eyes

I wish we could drink this way forever
But we're just hours from the sun
There's only room in this coffin for one
So much at stake, I can't fathom
That the world would let the living
Co-exist with phantoms
And we're just hours from the sun
If we can't dust together
One of us has to watch the other run

With these immortal eyes
There's something in the way we pain together
And how you want me to go on longer
Stop me from drinking holy water
I hold you and pray that God forgives
Two monsters who didn't choose to live like this

We're just hours from the rising sun
And for one of us, our time has come

There'd be no rush to get rich
We could rest for fifty years and
finally get the hang of it
I'd buy you a mansion in the darkest corners
of the world to explore with these immortal eyes
Other lovers are bound to forget
Every detail about the person
they're holding hands with
But I'd remember every survivor's wound
and breaths you draw
I observe with these immortal eyes
But the time has come
Only room in this coffin for one

Preacher Speaking

Preacher speaking about blessings but truth is
I'm barely eating
He's saying something about apples and Eden
But I'm spacing out
Grappling with the fact I'm starving
Can barely afford a pizza
Went to a priest, he recited the same thing
But a bit slower

Heaven feels farther so I keep on reaching
Grasping for straws, who'll draw the shortest?
Are we just lost in the woods
Seeking a specific tree in the forest?
Heard the most beautiful song
And I only noticed the chorus
The third time around
Too busy picking at the verses

What's it like to enter a palace?
The Hilton is the closest I've been to Paris
Who can I meet to bump up my status
Feeling a little less than average
I've never smoked a Cuban
And I'll never own the Mavericks
But mark these words
I'm marking my territory
No one else will write my tale
Or be the author of my story
So I came back the next week
And heard the preaching speaking

Everyone sees my outer flaws
Unaware of my inner demons

Turned to the woman next to me
Her makeup running
She lost everything she ever had
But she keeps on coming
Said every day she has breath in her lungs
Is a day she can use to right her wrongs
I sit there in silence as the band comes on
Observed the room while singing a song

No one any less or more than me
Praising a God we cannot see
Is life action or our reaction to what we're dealt?
I lent my ears to the words as I knelt
He spoke about blessings but the truth is
I've been taking them for granted
I woke up living at all
Even if I was living average

Passing Through

Found your plates on the interstate
Did you expect to pass the welcome sign
Were you coming in to buy some land?
Or just here for a good time?
I have a problem with getting attached
That when you leave town I hope you look back
Perhaps we had too many potholes and crumbling facades
But maybe the soul of the citizen will attract

Found your name written on the bathroom wall
A message written about the girls they never forgot
You're the only one who shares your name
Who's ever driven through this place
There are less people than there are parking lots
We can clean up the parks and better our mascot
But may it be the heart that you'll always see
Remember the good parts every time you leave
I wasn't always this polished from the start

A welcoming party for the twentieth time
Your face postered at the "Now Entering" sign
Were you coming in to buy some land?
Or just here for a good time?
Are you a tourist just passing through
Soaking in the skyline and forest views
I was hoping you'd stay this time
A new address to reside
For this heart has saved a room

Art by Rubin Baradi

...but we don't come around twice...

Who Drew These Maps?

It was a bad night so I slept instead
Two seats on the bus as my bed
The moon rises different in Tucson
Than where I'm from
Can't wait to leave as the sun
Beats down when morning comes
Fell asleep at midnight on Cali desert road
Woke up in Arizona where cactus grow

Do I need a map?
I'll just go where this train leads
And get off where my mind feels free
I can swing by a church in Texas heat
Pray to Jesus for Mary to meet me
'Cause right now I could use some roses and rosary
And a stranger to hold me motherly

I don't know where I'm going
Just that I need to go
Spent $50 on a hotel and trashed it
Discovered Miami felt nothing like Nashville
Maybe I should've danced salsa
Instead of played a country song
Then this sweet woman would cling to my arm

Drove a thousand miles to a new bar
Just to find myself alone
Then I came across another drifter
Who drove a thousand miles to see what gives
'Cause her hometown felt nothing like this

Something about this city is more alive
Did I bring it down when I arrived?

She assured me my sadness is an easy fix
When I toss the maps and just exist
Dance all night as the live band sings
Our bodies dry but the memories live
Who drew these maps anyway?

Took my journey to the Chesapeake Bay
The fish and crabs took the bait
And I left with my catch
En route to Philly
Maybe some brotherly love can fulfill me
Spend my days on cheesesteak and liberty
Hop the train to Portland, Maine
Thinking I was headed back west
But that's alright, the lighthouse caught my eye
Eat lobster by the coast before I rest for the night

Wake up in New York
Against the mainstream so I swim upstate
Question what I'm living for
The snow's got me dreaming of warmer towns
Wishing to be back in SoCal now

But then I sipped coffee black
In a Mid-American roadside
Where I made them locals laugh
And they shared with me their good times
Seven of us in a diner
Offers gentle reminders
The wheels can spin forever
And I'll never find what I don't know I desire

Maybe I'm just running from the bad times
And chasing the good byes
Wherever I've gone, I'll miss it
I tossed the maps and I just existed
I'm done running from the bad times
On my way to the good nights

Catching Trains

You're more North Hollywood
I'm more Downtown LA
Settled down pretty nicely
While I'm busy catching trains
But you stick around me
Try to ground me when things don't go my way
You're busy catching breaks
And I'm busy catching trains

So I'm here to say
Thank you
Nothing as lovely as that
I don't see myself reaching stations
But you keep me on this track
Thank you for steadying the line
I was headed southbound the entire time

She caught me at the train station
And said "don't forget where you're from"
Are you coming or are you going
Will you come or will you go
Part of life is not knowing

You're busy catching breaks
And I'm busy catching trains
And because of you
I'll reach the station someday

P.Y.A.

Step onto the stage
We sing those songs of faith
A whole congregation looking to me
For words to get them through the work week
The band wraps up, my mouth leads
And I don't know about the wars at home
Step off the stage
Missed calls throughout the day
Dial back with thoughts of small talk and pleasantries
But before I can speak
I hear "It's time to come home..."

I sing the songs every Sunday
Yet I still I find myself at his frail side
I read the Word today
We're going to war today
Holding his hand as he nears goodbye
The family still fighting this
Though it all feels dire
Fingers running through his hair
And we're sitting there
Fingers grazing pages of the bible
And we sang
We sang loud enough for the neighbors to hear
And they came
With words of hope despite the fears
And they joined the choir
Singing in the living room
As he bears a smile
And I recall when she called with the news

He's heading into the 4th stage
Just as I'm about to sing songs of faith

What does it mean to be a believer
When you can believe and still suffer?
Then I remember we all go through something
Same heartbreaks, just living in the body of another
His sentences shorten to words
Six months in, still fighting this war
Guide him from the living area to his bed
Daily cries, daily prayers, daily bread
I usually have the words in situations like this
That's why they come to see me on Sundays
We sit in silence
Know what it means to be quiet
And she says "we Praise You Anyway"

Headed back to work
I preach about human pain
But I'm the one hiding the hurt
They step onto the stage
And sing those songs of faith
My eyes trace the room and observe
What lies behind these singing faces?
Who here dwells in much worse places?
They leave these four walls into a scary world every day
And they Praise You Anyway

Just when I can breathe for a second
A call comes in from her
Watch it ring as the band sings your name
I finally accept
Yes, I finally accept it
Just found out he's reached his worst days

And in two minutes I have to preach
Tell them about how good You are
"Come back home and prepare a new song"
I sing the songs every Sunday
Yet I still I find myself at his bedside
I read the word today
We're going to war today
Holding his hand as he nears goodbye
We sing his favorite songs
Hallelujahs and amens
Loud enough for the neighbors to return again
The lyrics won't heal him
But they give him a different feeling
We know it could be any day
Closes his eyes and he Praises You Anyway

Losing a battle isn't losing a war
When you lose a loved one
But still have loving words
Button up my shirt and go back to work
To be human is to hurt
But a number of us know it's not the end
Back on the stage again
Worship team sings and I join them
Lyrics won't rewrite history
But it gives a different acknowledgement
It could be any day
And I'll Praise You Anyway

From A Distance

He watches her live for cameras
From a distance in his beat up sneakers
He can't get passed the barricade
Wishing he could somewhat be her
Maybe then he can treat his family
Endless vacations and summer days
He's been at this for fifteen years
and never once caught a break

She watches the world from all angles
Everybody wants to move in close
Having to love everyone is her disadvantage
How is there room for those she loves most?
He doesn't think she sees him
But she spots him from behind designer shades
Secretly she wants to be him
Because she's been at this for fifteen years
and never once had a break

Owns the world under her red bottoms
Marking down dreams and crushing goals
She prefers to wear cheaper sneakers
And live a life that doesn't crush her soul
Owns nothing but sand beneath rock bottom
Marking down dreams so far, so close
He prefers to be where people truly see him
And be in world that cares when he goes

He's stuck way up in nosebleed seats
She's living it up with the court side crowd
The cameras see him just as filler

They zoom in on all her fillers
She's stuck questioning what is real
All this money and she still gets shit for free
He paid tickets just to watch a screen
Every five seconds they cut to her on TV

He watches her live for cameras
From a distance in his beat up sneakers
The world watches her from all angles
And she can't smile until the cameras leave her

By Choice

Been single for seven years
But it wasn't by choice
It's just matter of timing
And not being someone's choice
That's alright, the economy's not on my side
They're out there driving lemons, I'm getting by on my Limes
Been at this for several years
I guess it's my choice
To author papers instead of stapling them together
At some office with a corner view
You can't always choose who loves you
But you can choose what to create
I've had more luck writing stories
Than scoring dinner dates
The beauty to art is not having to explain
Everything you're saying
But they hear it and feel it a thousand different ways
Words floating off pages, I pray they heal someone's pain
I'm no bible writer but may it change them the same

The Before/The After

Tuesday morning comes around
A quiet day, a little too quiet
Without warning, something earth shattering
Shakes the ground
The birds keep chirping
The ants keep building
But we stop to run to the nearest television
So many words and confusion and sounds

Tuesday morning comes around
We're sipping on coffee, sitting on stools
Talking to two million viewers about celebrity news
It's my job to be composed
But how can I think straight
When it explodes on live TV
And my family's blowing up my phone
Asking if I'm okay
We're cutting to commercial break
What do I say?
I've got two minutes to deliberate
Rush to the green room
Stomach bursting in sickness
From seeing things no human should witness

Tuesday morning comes around
I'm rushing through traffic to make it to town
Get to work twenty minutes later for the twentieth time
They decide it's finally time for me to be fired
I say my goodbyes to my cubicle and friends
Thinking of what I would tell the wife and my kids

A moment of freedom, the sky crystal clear
Just to watch my old workplace crumble in the rearview mirror

Tuesday morning comes around
I'm definitely failing this test
Last night was for studying
But I was glued to TV sets
My teacher interrupts, pencils down now
A tremble in her voice and eyes to the ground
"I'm sorry to tell you there's been an attack"
Wasn't expecting this in sixth grade math class

Tuesday morning comes around
Hours in the delivery room
There's a rush of new patients a hallway down
"Didn't you hear the news?"
A day forever captured
She won't know what it's like before
What will the world be like hereafter
For my baby just born?

Tuesday morning comes around
Something was lost but more things were found
Two fighting neighbors at war over fences
Two pairs of couples arguing over expenses
Bickering quickly drinking daily brew
When one neighbor tells the other to put on the news
They sat in a living room to hear about war
Two couples, four neighbors night fighting anymore

Microphone

I forget how young you are
Where we see burnouts
You see stars
The world is your oyster
We just have the shell
You've got a pearl that I've never held
You don't know how good you are
It's winter and you're still at the summer job
Ringing up orders then off you go home
You don't know you'd do so well with that microphone
Quit your day job at the pizza spot
Don't rob yourself of the day dream
Watch out who's in your corner
Same jerseys don't mean the same team
Scraping up pennies to get your weekend vice
That's nice
Well, time flies by so if I were you I'd
Realize how good you are
Let go of how dumb you've done life
We're all smart enough to figure it out
We make it through but don't get it twice
Ten dollars can get to six figures somehow
If you start right now
You don't know how good you are
It's winter and you're still at the summer job
Ringing up orders then off you go home
You don't know you'd do so well with that microphone

Young Holly Would

Holly stood alone in the hall to run some lines
Powder on her cheeks and dressed to the nines
With just a few minutes to go
Until she meets the head of her favorite studio
She's 36 but the role reads 25
Might be the last chance to keep her career alive
Thinks of mom and dad and
how proud they'd be
To finally see baby girl on the TV screen

Secretary peeks out and calls her in
Leaves her alone as the meeting begins
Something about the vibe in the room
Has her stomach sinking in
Small talks of movies and favorite shows
Something about family and hometown blues
A silence in the room with no one around
Holly watches the clock as the minutes count down

He has blow spread across the table top
But she asked the secretary for water not coke
Holly didn't want to be a bother
She politely declined, before another
sentence was spoke
Might as well applied for an entry level job
Because there'd be a different male in the room
There's a line of women wrapped
around the corner
For a conversation that could've
been done on Zoom

He's getting himself comfortable
slipping off his coat
Loosening the buttons from his
expensive dress shirt
All of the monologue leaves Holly's memory
As he name drops celebrities just to impress her
He comes up behind her to slip off her jacket
Mentions it's getting warm in the office
"How much do you really want to be an actress?
So many of you go back home jobless."

Hands caress her shoulders a little too long
Says to relax because it's really "nothing that wrong"
"Have a bump with me
Forget the monologue
Sit on my lap and dance
And you secure the job"

Then she realizes she's been:
Called her into the room to run some lines
Powder on her nose and fear in her eyes
This is not what she signed up for
But what so many others lined up for
A single moment that defines her career
Decades of training and dedication to get her here
Rises from her chair because she knows her worth
He says "if you tell anybody you'll never find work"
She smiles and simply states "we'll see"
Picturing mom and dad watching her on TV
Walks away from the office as she should
Good thing she's a bit older
Because who knows if young Holly would

lonely pLAce

Everyone thinks I'm doing fine
Just because I have execs on speed dial
Someone told me I'm next in line
Well, that line's wrapped around the corner store

I feel the pressure, I feel out of place
It's just something about LA
Fight temptation and fight fate
Fight loneliness living among the 8's and more
I've been lost 'cause
Maybe I'm a lost cause
I was given the ball and played the wrong sport
I gave out my number
Turns out she wanted to be an extra
If they all want to work, then who's left for me to court?

The suit and ties at steak dinner
I couldn't even get past the host
I blew up her phone when I got fitter
I lost my spirit so I guess she had to ghost
They've got stacked rosters from the apps
Pretty sure I lost my appetite
Just when I thought I've hooked them
No one ever bites
I feel the pressure, I feel the pain
It's something lonely about this pLAce
She's a good get and I won't regret her
But over time she said "I miss the old you"
Her heart drew cold as I sipped my cold brew
Maybe just to counter the weather

Everyone thinks I'm doing fine
But 'fine' is pinned to my window wiper
Too many signs to read for a part time driver
I hate this city but I love it partly
Because I like the people but don't vibe with the policies
I feel the pressure, I feel the pace
Figure out a way to make a dollar today
I feel tethered, I feel the weight
There's just something about this pLAce

Doctor Said

I quit cigarettes but you're still in my lungs
Doctor said that's what I get for the fun
I quit my favorite drinks and favorite pubs
But doctor said you're still in my blood
That's what I get for hanging on
To something not good for the first,
Second, or third run
Like when we'd sneak out on Monday nights
Daddy took the keys so we'd hitch a ride
So we couldn't enjoy the dropdown
Talk about the good times in town
That were a waste of time
I cut out sugar and mostly salt
Doctor said I'm healthier overall

But there's still damage to my system
Didn't like what I heard so I didn't listen
And went back for the fourth go round
Maybe it'll be different if I keep persisting
We ran out on date night
Didn't pay the bill since we didn't get the hype
Went to jail on a first strike
Talk about the waste of a first time
To realize I was only short a dime

I should probably live differently
But I can't read what the doctor wrote
I didn't like what I had to hear
So I took his pad and penned my own note

Sent Me a Storm

He sent me a storm to test my faith
And I hid in a house till the rain passed
He sent me a drought to test my soul
And I stole my neighbor's water and kept his glass

I told everyone I had belief
But if they saw my belief through a microscope
What would they think of me if they'd likely see
I'm a bit more hype than hope

There's probably a lesson here
If only I didn't sleep through school
I see him everywhere
But barely speak to the principal

Enough Fists

I preferred you in politics
And they threw their stones and sticks
Which I used to build a home instead of bricks
Canceled by my friends when I say your name
Said I should separate you from the state
But doesn't shyness mean I'm ashamed?
If I call on you in sadness and silence
But fear bringing you up to them?

They thank God at the podium without knowing Him
Then every other day live different
I suppose we're meant to take the dirt
Anything that bears your name will share the hurt
Maybe you'll see who runs the race with you
Instead of crowning who comes in first

The TV called me crazy
As did my neighbors down the hall
They call me many things I don't claim
Instead of not calling me at all
I just want the simple things
But the funny thing about human beings
Preach to me about women's rights
But can't tell me what a woman is
Then there are days with fits of rage
The mud on my face gets mixed with rain
Stuck outside with oncoming thunderstorms
Questioning what I'm fighting for
Dirt underneath my nails
I put in grit and I still fail

At getting to where I want to be
On this slow road walking with you
God, where'd you go?
I don't have a enough fists to shake up high
I looked for you on the skyline
Where the red and orange separate
Who hired you? You did your job wrong
I took a step back and thought
Wait, that's not how this works
God, where'd I go?
I used to have more faith than this
I took a step forward and watched
The sun return as I released my grip

I spoke up about the recent break-ins
They turned their heads and called me racist
As if I had control over who the suspects are
I want my children to be raised in the safest places
They snatched up purses and Northfaces
And somehow they blame the store owners
For setting up shop where they are
Broken heaters and leaky faucets
I don't have money, in my eyes
But times are tough and we have to monetize
And somehow I'm the fool
For voting for the guy who'd put more money in our pockets

Woke preachers painting a different Jesus for them likes
He'd sit at your table but wouldn't vote for your vice
But yes, he wouldn't love the sinner any less
Progress is a nice word for changes with no end
God, where'd you go?
I don't have a enough fists to shake up high

I looked for you on the skyline
Where the red and orange separate
Who hired you? You did your job wrong
I took a step back and thought
Wait, that's not how this works
God, where'd I go?
I used to have more faith than this
I took a step forward and watched
The sun return as I released my grip

Make friends on earth but endgame is God
Incline your ear to me, hear my words
Wondrously show your steadfast love
Remind me of what I'm bleeding for
Down here is maybe meant to be a losing war
Only have two fists to fight culture

Bullets for Breakfast

Walking dead at moonlight
I'm really feeling helpless
I can't down these eggs
I want bullets for breakfast
All the bullies and hecklers
I'm gonna do something reckless
Maybe this belt will hurt less
Than this diamond necklace
Ceiling fan's my only support system
Won't these pills dissolve quicker
Want evidence? Here's your proof
Add vodka to the mixture
Here's the absolute truth
I'm calling down the contacts
I'm giving them five to ten minutes
For at least one to call back

Dialing A to Z, already at my exes
Lost hope when I breezed through the Christians
And left two voicemails for Jesus
Everyone wants to know why
I'm blowing up their messages
Just after midnight
I hit up Zee and my mind is made
They will see what happens
We're all zombies anyway
And this is target practice
And I can't help but think
It's just anxiety
I'm blindly walking the darkness idly
Edging on the brink

There's two minds inside of me
One says jump into bed
The other wants me to fall
Face first in the pavement below
Wow, look at him go
Cement myself in history
The news quick to approach
Putting an end to my misery
Crowds form, isn't that the norm?
See him for what he is at death
Never for what he was before

I'm beside myself
Like this revolver on the shelf
What's the resolve to this
Who do I call for help?
No apologies, no note left behind
My cursive's illegible
These curses are buried inside
Standing on this ledge again
No one will let me in
Walking a razor thin line
Is this the best a man can get?
Drenched in pounds of sweat
Did I put the rounds in yet?
I'm calling down the contacts
I'm giving them five to ten minutes
The gun will get more heat than I do
After all, it's the year .22

They'll learn my name for a minute
Before someone else wants to become more famous
I bought bullets for breakfast
I've come to my senses

Innocent civilians listen to the laws, but I'm not civil
Leaving them defenseless
When will they learn their lesson?
They'll never listen
They won't blame it on me
Shaking their fists at the weapon
No one to stop me, boys in blue defunded
And armed protectors told to sit on the benches
I'm dining alone, give me all the glory
See my face on rotation for a million news stories
They won't wonder how I got here, from a boy to a monster
Bought bullets for my bullies but decided to go further
It doesn't have to happen
But something finally snapped
You can have red flags
But you can't find me on the map

Walking dead at moonlight
I'm really feeling helpless
It's the night before it happens
Will someone pick up before breakfast?

Love of Girl/Love of God

I wanted to write a love song to girl
But I instead I wrote one for God
I've only met one of the two here on earth
But only one has shown to love me first
Two lines intersected in ink on my arm
Set up a shrine to someone like a ghost
Well, a lack of presence defines her too
As much as I try to keep my eyes on Him
My eyes keep running back to you
Brush off all the women around town
And forget all the ones in the digital space
Devote an hour to prayer as if He's sitting there
But I can't even put a face to a name
Turn my attention to her essence across the room
Brimming with beauty, peace, and solitude
Tripping over words while trying to read this bible verse
Then I remember who loved me first
Reset my gaze on these pages
Somewhere between Genesis and Revelations
But I lift my face to catch her stare
And latched to the one I could see right there
The seat I saved for my Savior
Is now the spot I mistakenly gave her
Shut the book on the table
And in that second I cut my losses
For an hour she doesn't leave
In my head I pray He's forgiven me
Then she bears witness to my ink and rolls up her sleeve
We've two tattoos of matching crosses

Never Broke a Heart

Fifteen to my name
I don't know where I'll sleep tonight
Downtown LA is not where to be
If you've never learned to fight
But if I got grit and don't give a shit
I'll get by before close
Sit in a cafe for hours
And do everything in my power
To make another few dollars on my phone

Can living like this hurt if I don't feel worth?
Got my good health and broke in shoes
I've saved money on dinner
Just by eating for one
Even if starving for two
Everybody's dining with someone
Somehow I never got that far
Can I say I know how to love
If I never broke a heart

Tonight I'll lay my head on a king-sized bed
All this space to myself without a queen
Rounded up a hundred bucks or so
Wired on coffee shop cappuccino
And now I'm too awake to sleep
Maybe I'd always have a place to lay
If I made connections at the bars
Can I say I know how to love
If I never broke a heart

Barely slept a minute as the morning hits

Guess it's time for round two
Hit the cafe to find another roof
Split my time between lattes at Verve and wraps at Spitz
Maybe I'd have a default mattress
If I'd fall in love with some actress
But does romance live in these parts?
I'd start tonight if there was a travel guide
Could I ever really love
If I don't even know a broken heart?

The Dreamer comes and goes...

Too Soon

Just when I thought I got to the party too soon
The second to arrive was more than words could articulate
Doors open in slow motion
Hair in the wind, a smile to relight the sun
A choir singing in my head
Forced conversation between two early birds
Who'd never connect if someone else came earlier
We joked and laughed all night
As if no one else was around
Then midnight struck
And she had to skip town
My guts said don't do it
It'd look too desperate
She just took off and
I'm already chasing her to the intersection
A slip of the lips said "I'd like to see you again"
I pulled the trigger too soon
She wasn't ready for someone like me
And off to the airplane she went

Four months pass, another season wraps its working hours
And just by chance there she is
The second to the party of this barren coffee shop
Share a tiny laugh as our eyes match
She gives into fate
Of all the hipster cafes, she walks into mine
Through all the espressos, she'll give me a shot
Steady life, steady as we go
Sharing a car and our first home
The gifting of tickets to faraway places
It lights up her face to a God-like hue

Talks of futures and what-if scenarios
I'm just happy anywhere she goes
As long as anywhere isn't the last destination
Because right now that's a bit too soon
But fate will be fate
And I got the call
Something about crossing the intersection
Get to the hospital now or don't come at all
There she is
My beauty wrapped up in tubes
Hours of I love you's
Then God took her home too soon

My friends play their part
But I can't leave this room
An addition of wrinkles and cigarettes
Zoned out stares and untrimmed hair
I grip to the sheets where she used to sleep
Who needs washing when you've got my tears?
They wait for me by the doorway
To ensure I don't do anything stupid
But I sit and glare and just ignore them
Maybe loving at all is what's foolish

Four weeks go by, another month wraps up its working hours
Can I laugh or is it too soon?
What's the length of time it takes?
Another rotation from the moon?
It won't be long, I'll smile again
You were my centerpiece, a centerfold
Now I'm packing boxes of your folded clothes
Gathering pictures of all our moments
If I knew this day would come so soon
I'd clutch you closer

I remember you dearly
Just when I thought I got to the party too soon

The second to arrive was more than I deserved
I saw you in slow motion
Hair in the wind, a smile to relight the sun
A choir singing in my head
Forced conversation between us two
Led me to be the one to spend this time with you
We wouldn't get later, but are blessed we got soon

Longing for Drought

Have you spent a year in the rain
That you're longing for drought?
You no longer feel home
In your own hometown
Until the day you get lost
Just another in the crowd
The old bed that you left
Is what you're wishing for now

Was a big fish in a small pond
Then the pond dried up
Thought I was way too good for the neighborhood club
Then they replenished the water
And everyone swam there
I didn't how to float so I would just stand there
Have you spent a year in that rain
That you're longing for drought?
You no longer feel home
In your own hometown
Until the day you get lost
Just another in the crowd
The old bed that you left
Is what you're wishing for now

Was a small fish in a big pond
Then the pond filled up
And it only got bigger when we weathered the flood
So we search for different water
And everyone came
A city with much sun but not so much rain

A year ago they had more hair
Mom and dad don't fair so well
Walking up the stairs
Need to spend more time spending time
Money comes and goes
But the people aren't always there
Have you spent a year in that rain
That you're longing for drought?
You no longer feel home
In your own hometown
Until the day you get lost
Just another in the crowd
The old bed that you left
Is what you're wishing for now

Art by Rubin Baradi

At the End of a Dream

I see the damage on your hands
You've worked your whole life
I promise to make things easy
I'll get rich and help you retire
Packed some boxes and a suitcase
I'll be back on the holidays
Months from now I'll mail a check
And we'll take the trips we never been

Moved to the big city with big dreams
And you can tell on the phone
Five months in, I went all in
I can't pay the rent and lost the home
That's okay, I'll bounce back
A year from now we'll think and laugh
About the days I lost the lights
To keep the faith and the hope alive

There we are
On top of the world
Everything we got we worked toward
After all these years you can finally rest
And I can say I gave the best of me
Meet me where we go at the end of a dream

I see the graying on your hair
Just want you to enjoy life
I promise to make things easier
I'll get rich and make you smile
Give your working hands a break
I don't know how long this will take

Just say a prayer and have some faith
I'll pay every penny back some day

I met the right people in my field
Won't we give it a bit more time
I promise it won't be another year
Just a few miles from the finish line
Hold on a little longer
Get you that mansion on the coast
We'll have plenty time to celebrate
I don't care what your doctor wrote

There we are
On top of the world
Everything we got we worked toward
After all these years you can finally rest
And I can say I gave the best of me
Meet me where we go at the end of a dream

Things took a turn, slight delay
Met a partner I could see me wed
We were in love till the love went away
And I'm back on my own to pay this rent
Didn't go as planned but I'm getting by
I have another interview next week
Maybe it'll land on year five
It'll make sense and you'll finally see
This is it, I'm waiting for the call
Sorry you had to sit this long
I see the wearing in your eyes
As you keep the faith and the hope alive

There we are
On top of the world

Everything we got we worked toward
After all these years you can finally rest
And I can say I gave the best of me
Meet me where we go at the end of a dream
We held on a little longer
A few more wrinkles on both our skins
Did you get the first deposit
Like I promised way back when
Let's hold on a little longer
My time here's coming to a close
I did what I said I'd accomplish
May you enjoy your views from the coast

Fans

On top of the world
She has a billion fans
Generations before her swept floors
To get her here
Blood, sweat, tears, perseverance
From zero in the bank account to six zeros
Everything she wanted she prospered
Food on the table for her mother and father
A trajectory that couldn't go any further
America's sweetheart
Treated like a queen
Gave back to the community
All over TV screens
Elevated others who looked like her
Many jobs to minorities
Put her own money into grants
Added a million other fans

Hang in there, superstar
She's hanging in there

She walked with the people
Born into lower class
Never claimed to be oppressed
And to work to afford the dress
She worked with the people
And not the elite
Who claim they work for the people
But see them as sheep
On top of the world
She has a billion fans

The mob created a new trend
And expected her to feel the same thing
See her views as insensitive
Her career is dependent
On whether or not
A billion people paint her opinion negative
Lost the backing of executives
Backlash came repetitive
In a time where they preferred feelings over facts
She fell from the top and lost a billion fans

Hang in there, superstar
She's hanging in there

They turned against her in droves
Picketed outside her home
Got her mother fired from her job
And wrote her father's number on the highway wall
Their leaders said to go high
But they couldn't stoop any lower
Supporters stuck around in hopes of
Her career getting another go
On top of trending topics
She lost a billion fans
Family tries to lift her up anyway that they can
Boyfriend shows up knowing she's still reeling
Reaches her door and gets a sinking feeling
Turns the knob to find her
Hanging from the ceiling fan

Hold on, superstar
She's holding on

A few months in recovering

Bruises fading from her neck
Blood still drips from the knives in her back
From lost fans, friends, and "fact checks"
They let her go from the scene
Just to be picked back up
By a population who feels the same way
Who were all told to pack up
They never went away
Only to come rise stronger

Hang in there, superstar
She's hanging in there

Went to Sleep

Went to sleep in my club clothes
Woke up in my church clothes
Either way every day
Is a hurt that God knows
Give it up to the DJ
Give it up to the pastor
Because of both of them
I got to church faster

Went to sleep in a booth
Woke up in a pew
This section was for VIP
And now it's for the youth
All the security's gone
Greeted by the hosts in line
Got drunk off vodka and lime
Now filled with God and Jesus wine

Went to sleep in my sheep clothes
Woke up in my wolf clothes
My body's at the same address
But Sundays I wear a different soul
In search of happiness
The madness takes its toll
Went to sleep in the sadness
But today I woke up at all

Twenty Years Part I

Worked an office job
Like running a marathon
This autumn he finally made a partner
Got his wife everything she ever wanted
And everything she never did
Wasn't always in the form of a dollar
She stood by him when he was close to getting fired
Together twenty years and watched him struggle
Stayed long hours just to heat up the apartment
And feed the children and get through the hardships
Walked him in to the bus stop when he couldn't afford a car
Kissed him goodbye everything morning
Knowing it wouldn't always be like this
Knowing they wouldn't always grieve like this
Cheered him on from the front row as she tended to the kids
For twenty years she did

When he'd come home feeling little
And she reminded him life could change in an instant
Hitting six figures isn't so simple
One hundred thousand dollars starts off with a single
Worked an office job
He ran a marathon
That autumn he finally made a partner
But that summer she lost him
Got his wife everything she ever wanted
And all she wanted was her husband back
She knows victory but has her share of losses
Prayed to God for an offer to have her husband back

Dressed a year in all black

Clothing and emotions matched
Beers and cigarettes by the pack
For twenty years she stared at watches
What she'd give to wait up and see him come home from the office
Twenty years to get the family here
Even on nights he put the business first
Last autumn he finally made partner
And right now she was missing hers

Truly Lived

He spent his life away from water
Too afraid to swim and get swallowed
Up by the sharks swarming
So he locked himself up in a tiny room
Nothing but a small window for a view
For many decades he existed, but he never truly lived

He spent his life away from flights
Too afraid to course through skies
Up where lighting and thunder form
So locked himself up in a tiny room
Nothing but a small window for a view
For so long he existed, but did he ever truly live?

He spent his life away from romance novels
Because maybe one day he want a story
Only to have his heart get stomped on
So locked himself up in a tiny room
Nothing but a small window for a view
For so long he existed, but did he ever truly live?

Caught his reflection, gray hair and wrinkled cheeks
Maybe now's the time to take a peak
Cracked the door open to glance outside
More beauty than his window could provide
Others swam the oceans and soared the skies
And maybe endured heartbreak sometimes
Only to end up fine
And truly lived

Goodbye, California

Goodbye, California
You had all this time to meet me
Now I have all this time to kill
Would drive down the coast for the thrill of it
I could afford the views there more than Hollywood Hills
Goodbye to late night runs with friends
Take a ride down Sunset and see stars at both ends
Goodbye to empty pockets till I come back again
You can't paint without pain
That's where the art begins

I can trade golden bridges for eastern bays
Even if I'd miss Silver Lake on most days
There's a magic in missing out on what they post when I'm gone
How could I lose what wasn't mine all along?
Goodbye California
I can dream from anywhere
And anywhere lets me down softer
Goodbye California
I promise to give you space
Even if I were to visit often
Go solo at SoHo
And leave with a supermodel
We can dream, can't we?
Because waking has gotten harder
Broke doesn't mean broken
I just underestimated a little what it means
To live under your means
Every penny towards keeping the lights on
Instead of shooting your drama
Drink all night till I'm a drunken stoop

My liver don't like me
But my lovers do

Goodbye California
I just need 100 proof
That if I drink your wine again
I won't get a hard time at second chances
Like Viners do
Goodbye California
I'll take silver in your golden state
California Dreams, for now I cannot sleep
"Hello again" will have to wait

...but the dream doesn't need to die...

Stop Looking

This was the place I was once knew
A long time ago it was new once
Got my name here
Family found their place here
Can't let go of the city where I grew up
To the world it's a photo opp
To me it's my home
It's time to stop looking for where I belong
We never stop growing up
But there's a choice in not going alone
It's time to stop looking for it's with you I belong

Now there's that smile I once knew
A long time ago it was new once
From the summer you met me
Something about this we can't forget
Won't let go of the love where I felt good enough
To the world it's a photo opp
To me it's my home
It's time to stop looking for where I belong
We never stop growing up
But there's a choice in not going alone
It's time to stop looking for it's with you I belong

A Love Story

You can't sell dreams but you can sell crimes
Sold your soul just to sell rhymes
Busy your nostrils, reimbursed by jail time
Wrecked in the record but your records sell fine
Pose for blogs though barely famous
Internet houses you but internally you're vacant
Paychecks changed you but your sense barely came
So close to sober but you chose to marry Jane
A death in the chapel after the black wedding
From meth in the lab to rehab and drab settings
Exchanged God for fame, lured by possession
Pocket full of change but like a church without blessings
Devil on the shoulder you codenamed conscience
Deposited Jackson atop Washington
And hallucinating presidents
Pride in your eyes bordered on self-obsession
Empty in your heart like first appearance without impression
Went from that hood rich to that Good Rich
Hop on that Michelin
Finally afford the Ford to Escape
Detroit, Michigan
Hungry for more placements
LA bound and thirsty
Putting faith in the wrong places
Lambo have mercy
You can't sell dreams but you can cell crimes
Sold your soul just to sell rhymes
The Man and The Dollar
A love story to stand the test of time

Day Dream

I know
I've been this way since eighteen
Left with nothing but a suitcase and a dream
So many lakes and rivers that I crossed
So many corners from the pictures that I cropped
Don't think
I'm not suffering
But I'm way too drunk off this day dream
You said, "Sit still and think straight"
But who am I to leave it up to fate?
I'm too young to burn out quick
Meant to outlast your favorite pack of cigarettes

I know
I'm far from home
But my home is where you go
Day dream
You've seen
I've been this way once before
When I followed my favorite artist on tour

Swore one day I'd be on the A-team
Set back by days that I've been wasting
Don't think
I'm not suffering
But I'm way too drunk off this day dream
You said, "Don't move, just think this through"
But my world is bigger than that room
I'm too young to burn out quick
Meant to outlast your favorite pack of cigarettes

I know
I'm far from home
But my home is where you go
Day dream
You said, "You can always come back to your hometown"
But I'm in too deep to turn around
I can't go wrong on a one way road
And this drive's too fast to ever slow down
I'm too young to burn out quick
Meant to outlast your favorite pack of cigarettes

I know
I'm far from home
But my home is where you go
Day dream

If Walls Could Talk

If walls could talk, I'd tell you of the girl with the guitar wearing
bell bottom jeans. Her free-spirited eyes believe this city
will make her. As her pen hits her diary, she writes of fairy tales and love stories,
hoping this city doesn't break her.
I'd tell you of her sweet voice
humming to new Eagles and Fleetwood.
There's a poster pinned to me of Stevie Nicks.
She wishes she could be her.
Two years in, her smile fades.
Twenty songs in with no one to listen.
She set her sights on Hollywood but she lacked vision.

If walls could talk, I'd recite her phone calls to mom. Her eyes roll right when
she says "nothing's wrong." She paces the floor back and forth
as her mascara runs.
Twenty songs in with no one to sing along.
I'd sing back if somebody could listen.
She walks circles, humming her newest melody
before deciding it's not good enough.
Deciding *she's* not good enough.
Deciding one day she had enough.
If walls could talk
I would've stopped her.
Instead, I had to watch her.
I'd scream for some to restrain
her as a hundred pills left its container.

If walls could talk, I'd tell you
of the man in the denim jeans and mohawk,

laughing in the halls after sweet pleasantries
with his neighbors. But as soon as his door shuts,
he drops to the floor, rivers flowing from his eyes as
he downs his first bottle of the night.
Three years ago, he thought he'd live his dream.
Today, he has no clue what he's chasing.
First time living alone, he needed reflection.
Spent his days binging Harold Ramis
but he lacked direction.
The world below, he stared in amazement.
A brand new era under Reagan.
Everybody ran circles around him.
What was he chasing?
First time alone, he sought redemption.
Stripped me bare and painted me over.
Bold tones of yellow, red, and orange long gone as a white
glossed me entirely, like a blank canvas for him.

If walls could talk,
I'd have a conversation.
He'd down a pack a night
but not from celebration.
I wish I could hug the man in the denim.
So does the ghost of the girl in the bell bottom jeans who
watches from the corner.
He'll never notice her. She'll never notice me.
He offers one last look
before leaving me forever, luggage in hand,
adorned in Kiss stickers.
If walls could talk, I'd tell you about
the gentleman in the
Kangol hat and Adidas sneakers,
every night practicing rhymes
in the mirror. He pictures a crowd of 20,000 staring back at him.

But tonight it's just his walkman,
his dreams, and his fears.
He pictured himself with a career that was much better,
but there already lived a Prince the people thought was fresher.
He hoped his rhymes would some day work,
so he didn't have to smell of burgers and fries right after work.
One day a girl comes along and this studio finally
resembles a happy home. He told her someday
he'd move them to the Hills
for better views. His rhymes were getting better too.
But she didn't know what he got addicted to,
and if I could talk I'd tell her, too.

I'd tell you about the night he lined up snow
on the table and inhaled
more than he could handle.
Much more than he could before.
His eyes fell to the back of his head
a minute too long.
His girlfriend stepped in five
minutes too late.
I'd tell you how she dialed 9-1-1 at 7:31,
and the ambulance finally arrived
15 minutes after 8.
They rushed him out on a gurney,
and the music faded then.
That was the last I ever saw of him.

OVER BLACK, naive footsteps enter the room,
a sigh of relief acknowledging restored hope.
Open on...an ACTRESS, 20's, frosted tips
and a Britney sweater.
She puts down her bags and picks up a script.
Her slender hands can barely handle its weight.

As she recites lines
in the mirror, it's evident to me, an audience of one:
She's in ninth grade theater at best.
Maybe that's all it takes.
I've seen the big shots on the TV screen.
Pretty faces who can scream.
She compares herself to them all,
skipping on breakfast and lunch to
match the one on the poster.
It's Saturday night and she's staying in,
rehearsing lines in monotone execution.
At least she's better than last time. But as soon as reaches
an emotional climax, she loses it, flopping onto her springy mattress
in frustration.
Imperfection is the death of her.
If she doesn't nail this role,
she has to fly home, at least that's what she
promised daddy on the phone.
Tonight is the fifth glass she's thrown at me,
wallowing in self-doubt.
She takes a moment to breathe,
leaning her face against me and staining
me with her lipstick.
She's so over the ramen stacked in the corner.
The broken AC says it's time
for her to land a gig.
It's been hitting ninety-eight degrees.
The bills piling up on the counter
aren't fan mail. So she goes again.
Getting to that peak I'm looking for...
then she loses it.
Maybe she hasn't hurt enough,
not at this young age.

Where's the heartache, the angst, the rage?
Then, one day it came.

Glued to the screen on this September day.
Her kitchen phone reaches as far
as it can into the sleeping space,
shaking in her hands as she watches with trepidation
her mother on the other end.
"What plane was daddy on again?"
And there it is, the performance I've been looking for.
She drops to her knees, fists clenched,
bawling into her Backstreet sweater.
The voice of her mother equally pained,
letting me know the
talent runs in the family. The TV crashes to the floor
for extra measure. Maybe a bit heavy-handed,
but I'll take it.
Two days later, she'd walk out on me.
Wish I knew why, but I'm just a wall.

If walls could talk, I'd tell you about the man in the
ripped jeans and guitar.
His free-spirited eyes believe this city
will make him.
Glued to his phone at every second,
endless postings and notifications.
He strums his strings live for the world to see.
A million people notice him.
If walls could talk, I'd detail how jealous the ghost in the corner is.
A plate falls in the kitchen but he's too busy
streaming to notice it.
But she digresses. A tough pill to swallow
but the world today
is not like the one she lived in.

If walls could talk, I'd tell you how a song
that changed the world
was written in this 600 square foot studio.
I'd tell you about the call
from his agent that changed his life forever,
just hours after
he received the worst news ever,
but how his life is about to get better.
As he packs his suitcase to go off
to somewhere grander,
I admit I wish I got to know him.
Every second was a performance
with every moment of his life recorded.
But good for him that he made it.
Luckily, the city didn't break him.
As he streams his final exit,
the ghost in the corner is all but faded.

Here I am alone again with my memories
as my only friend.
Perhaps another will take residence.
A hundred thousand more stories
to witness here
as long as somebody's listening.

Can You Tell Us What It's Like

We'd grow up and not talk about the things we do now
Maybe because heaven seemed like a distant town
Read the good book page by page
But it doesn't warn us at what age
We learn to know what it's like

Spent our days adding to the family album
But we'd make more if we knew the outcome
Looking through them page by page
Laughing at how we looked at younger ages
Do you remember what it was like?

We could think back on what should've done
Or make the most of the rest of our run
There's no such thing as getting out but going through
I'm doing work down here
So your name will be read for thousands of years
So I can tell them what it's like knowing you
A final destination for living things
Is it as we imagine in the most vivid of dreams
Can you tell us what it's like up there in heaven
Or maybe just wait till we see you then

I went through some hurt today
I waited through the pain and that's okay
If God intervened every time we cried
That's not faith, that's expectation

Writing down words I wish I would say
As if I could just send them to you anyway

I'll fold the note and pocket the paper
Call it faith that I can tell you them later

A final destination for living things
Is it as we imagine in the most vivid of dreams
Can you tell us what it's like up there in heaven
Or maybe just wait till we see you then

Lakes and Rain

We can talk for hours on what we missed
It's been a while, can I call you my friend?
Ten months back we couldn't speak like this
But there's always an end to beautiful things
I guess we had the urge to reminisce
It's been a while since you smiled, my friend
Will it hurt to pull in this close again?
I guess we're moving on to beautiful things

The difference between warmth and pain
Is how close you are from the flames

You're spending summer swimming the lakes
While it feels like I'm drowning in rain
Would it be okay to meet you halfway
All this had changed in an instant
Have to send you my love from a distance
You're spending summer swimming the lakes
While it feels like I'm drowning in rain

We can meet for minutes over drinks
Before you're called back into your life
Are there variations of happiness?
Because yours looks so much different than mine
I guess we had the urge to reminisce
It's been a while since you smiled, my friend

The difference between warmth and pain
Is how close you are from the flames

I could linger here all my nights with you
But at some point we have to air dry

You're spending summer swimming the lakes
While it feels like I'm drowning in rain
Would it be okay to meet you halfway
All this had changed in an instant
Have to send you my love from a distance
You're spending summer swimming the lakes
While it feels like I'm drowning in rain

Just remember the promise of death...

Records

These songs build my memories
Alanis during dinner
Fleetwood on the drive
Clapton in the afternoon
I still hear them all the time
Even with lyrics I can't recite
I love them because they remind
Me of you

Press play on The Bee Gees
Followed up by Jackson Browne
Blast them on surround sound
We can play these songs forever
Listen to them when you're not near
So wherever I am you are here
Thank you for the records

A beautiful sound rang through the house
Joan sings of Diamonds & Rust
With Henley on "Desperado" coming up
Then "The Load Out" right on cue
"How they danced in the courtyard"
Never booked Hotel California
But I think I'd like a room
Because I would think of you

Press play on The Eagles
Followed up by Jackson Browne
Blast them on surround sound
We can play these songs forever
Listen to them when you're not near

So wherever I am you are here
Thank you for the records

We can take a trip to Boston
Get lost in their music and
Turn to Floyd's "Dark Side of the Moon"
Never booked Hotel California
But I think I'd like the view
Because I would think of you, dad

Press play on The Eagles
Followed up by Jackson Browne
Blast them on surround sound
We can play these songs forever
Listen to them when you're not near
So wherever I am you are here

God Gave Us You

Opened my eyes like sunrise
To love and protection
I knew at first sight I'd be fine
Gave us more than names and complexion

Long days turned into late nights
Sacrificed these years and you do still
Even if many girls will leave my side
You never will

Lucky because we got a masterpiece in you
Beautiful because we're all just pieces of you
And I know it's not much to say it in song
How much I love that you're always my mom
This much is true
You think God gave you us
But really God gave us you

Close my eyes, it's late night
Shower you and dad with prayers
Tethered to the telephone
Whenever I'm not there
Always worried for me
Even when I say I'm doing fine
Wake up early from your dreams
Hoping I could live out mine

Lucky because we got a masterpiece in you
Beautiful because we're all just pieces of you

And I know it's not much to say it in song

How much I love that you're always my mom
This much is true
You think God gave you us
But really God gave us you
He saved the best and gave us you

So much I can't fit in a hook and a verse
All the life and love you've given us
Can't be put into words

And I know it's not much to say it in song
How much I love that you're always my mom
This much is true
You think God gave you us
But really God gave us you
He saved the best and gave us you

A Song to Brother

There goes our youth
Wrestling on beds and breaking them
Ink on our skin would've bothered mom and dad way back when
There goes the crew
With years come friends and losing them
Wrinkles on our skin from wisdom we didn't have back then

80's babies, they don't make them like us anymore
We've seen fads outdated
But some things don't change at its core

Brother, big brother
Wherever is home with you
Miles apart on different roads
Won't change our roles
Even when we see the coast from different views
Brother, my brother
This one is overdue
Wouldn't ask for another
Big brother

There goes the years
Wrestling with adulthood like adults would
Who would've thought life would be this hard way back when
But our moment has come
With dreams come goals and crossing them

There's nothing that beats my losses like watching you win
80's babies, no one around is much the same

The world keeps changing

But your blood's always in my veins
Brother, big brother
Wherever is home with you
Miles apart on different roads
Won't change our roles
Even when we see the coast from different views
Brother, my brother
This one is overdue
Wouldn't ask for another
Big brother

Some day you'll need me to lift some of the load
Wrestling with life, restless in mind
Worried on the path you go…
I'll meet you on that road

Brother, big brother
Wherever is home with you
Miles apart on different roads
Won't change our roles
Even when see the coast from different views
Brother, my brother
This one is overdue
Wouldn't ask for another
Big brother

February Girl

The first on the team
She plays the lead
Didn't see her coming
But can't wait to meet
Open her eyes when snow covers autumn leaves

One day I'll have one of my own
Hold her in my hands like she's my own
The first one on the team
She plays the lead

Even if I can't make every single game
You'll always share my own last name

'Cause you're our February girl
Given life out in the springtime
And birthed in valentine
Growing up on a different coast
Call me up, girl anytime
Don't forget that you're our February girl

The second month in
Surrounded by love
Feel the warmth of family
On winter sun
Won't need candy or flowers
When you're surrounded by us
And even on days we're not on the same page
You'll always share my blood and my last name

'Cause you're our February girl

Given life out in the springtime
And birthed in valentine
Growing up on a different coast
Call me up, girl, anytime
Don't forget that you're my February girl

Maybe someday there'll be more in the yard
For you to protect when you're left in charge
You'll scream at them in anger then laugh too
My job is done when you see them
The way that I look at you

Our February girl

Little Sister

There she goes
Little sister
Last one to enter the room
But the first on the scene
When we need her

There she goes
Baby sister
I blinked a bit too long and
She's no longer little

Threw on your work clothes and that's when I figured
I want to change the world by entertaining it
But you'll change the world by saving it

Nurse's outfit neatly pressed
Hung on the door of the room I once slept
Lay your head on the bed where I once dreamt
Walls dressed in postcards of where we've been

Be a better person than I ever could
I nurse a bottle, you nurse the world

I'll change the people by entertaining them
You stay awake long hours saving them

There she goes
Baby sister
I blinked a bit too long and
She's no longer little

Blue Room

We came in crying just a minute apart
Two different voices, had no choice in it
I was glued to you
The doctor said she would be at risk
Mom and dad said, "we have a choice in this"
And that night I came home with you

Matching outfits all through school
Years spent together in a room painted blue
There are so many things that set us apart
But of all the people I'm blessed it was you

The world can tell the difference
And sometimes I forget
What it means to be of the same set
Now with different clothes,
different goals, different friends
Even when everything appears brand new
We'll always have shared the blue room

Here we are touching two opposing oceans
Two different homes, I had a choice in it
I went with my dream to see it through
As we age and our memories betray us
One thing remains I would never trade
It's the night I came home with you

Four walls were too small for our plans to fit in
Had to go so we both grow from within
Destined for greatness once we arrived

The only pain is knowing
We won't leave at the same time

The world can tell the difference
And sometimes I forget
What it means to be of the same set
Through the years, distinct careers,
different motives, different friends
Even when everything appears brand new
We'll always have shared the blue room

Where the Hero Lives

Work long days just to make it home
All of us waiting at the table
As time goes on, there are less chairs
I'd keep them there if I were able

I'd shave off years to add to yours
Lolo, which part of heaven do you love to explore?
Is it everything you imagined
And exactly what you worked hard for
To get in the good graces of God, the angels, and saints
Is the grass like mint and the rivers like paint
Run your fingers through the water and make a masterpiece?
Don't have to hustle to keep up with currency
And save electricity?
Can you fly at will over pastures and hills?
Can you wish the waterfalls to flow still

And Lola, as you lay in morning dew?
Down here, we are getting through
Taking it one day at a time
Fighting the heat, fighting the cold
Still doing what we're told
So one day we can make it home to you

Down here, we're still trying to make it work
To avoid sickness, to avoid wars
Still wondering, "What was I brought here for?"
Just pit stops on our way back home to you

I'd shave off years to add to yours
Oh good friend, which part of heaven

Do you love to explore?
Sorry it was all cut short
Didn't see the car around the corner
But you'd hate your hair gray anyway
Live on forever in your favorite jeans
The one I got you when you turned twenty-three
You loved it so much you wear it everyday
Where there's no time or reason or date or place
I know things like this are delicate
You showed in that dream you visited
Spoke of clouds and songs and old friends
And that dog you loved when you were ten

Grandpa, down here, we're still moving along
Another dollar earned, another day gone
We were by the ocean and you came to mind
With every sunrise and fishing line
I'd love for you to see what I'm working on
Wait for me by the finish line
Still reeling from what goes on
Down here we hustle to make it home

Grandma, I'd shave off years to add to yours
Which part of heaven
Would you offer a tour?
We prayed so hard for a cure
So down here wouldn't be so much to endure
Is it beautiful when the angels swirl
And are the gates made of actual pearl
So many questions I want to know the answer to
Save it for when I make it home to you
Do you sing with the choirs?
I heard your voice last night

It was right before bed
Or was it just a memory playing in my head

I'd shave years to add to yours
There's so much heaven on earth to explore
Beneath the rubble and traces of other people's wars
But off you go where the heroes live
Lies beauty abundant where God forgives
Death doesn't defeat us
For there's just one road
When our work is done
We'll see you at home

...gives us meaning to life

AN ARTIST

I'm an artist to the full extent
So if I fail there goes the apartment
There goes the ability to eat for a week
And meeting up with friends who can afford the parking
Keep my head down and order water
They're celebrating life and downing vodka
I guess the hardships make the accomplishments grow fonder
Just wondering how can I go much longer
They're waiting for me to do something big
Had a few large interviews
And waited for something since
Shout out to my friends checking in
I got my bank statement
Lord, I need saving

I'm an artist to the full extent
Pulled apart by anxiety and debt
In the business of dealing with pain and regrets
Ending our days with tears and cigarettes
Spent a paycheck on an outfit that fits me
Filled the tank to cross the whole city
Called a day off and asked the boss to take pity
Just to get to the audition and the casting acted shitty
I'm an artist to the full extent
Another gig lost, there goes the apartment
Can't eat with the stars, I'm starving
Can't look at my parents' faces with the pain that I'm causing

Living a couch for a month
Let's see what happens next
Humbled by the replies on Bumble
For a guy who hasn't figured it out yet
"Catch flights, not feelings"

But they fall in love with money and appearance
Someone in the middle of struggle
Is not so appealing
Everyone talks to me for connections
I get it
But my day just started
Let me get through my breakfast
I want us all to win, not here to be selfish
But I can know everyone in Hollywood
Yet no one's invested

I'm an artist to the full extent
My stay here is extended
I'm not a roommate, just a long term guest
My friend's patience is impressive
Told him he's the first on my list
To thank when I've made it big
Rolls his eyes since it's the fifth time I've said it since meeting him
And just when I think it'll turn around
Wake up to find myself six hundred dollars down
Everyone thought by now I'd run this town
Turns out I'm just running myself into the ground
And that ground sees me laying face down in mud
A mix of doubt, sweat, tears, and blood
Just when three hundred hits the account today
I lose double that on some autopay

I'm an artist to the full extent
And my arms have reached as far they can
Family has things to take of now
But I can't help without throwing in some towels
All this time and nothing to my name
Somehow got a loan up to look up some planes
Booked the flight for tomorrow, it's time to go

Just when I get the call someone loves what I wrote

SHORE DRIVE

Took me out for a ride on Shore Drive
Passed by the hospital I was born in
Didn't know where we'd arrive
But he said it's time for exploring
My first home on the corner
And my first school a few blocks after
That spot where I saw a student get bullied
Then surprised him with friendship and laughter

Took me out for a ride on Shore Drive
Asked me if every day was well spent
Giving joy and happiness
Because years are on short supply
And sometime soon we'll end this ride
Drove right by my first heartbreak
We turned eighteen on different paths
Realized I was under wrong influences
As we speed by this overpass

Took me out for a ride on Shore Drive
Caught the store where I worked
For a few dollars and nothing more
But it was the best summer of my life
I asked him to drive quicker
To pass the graves grandma and pa sleep
Was too busy with life to say goodbye
On the day before each would leave
Took me out to cruise down Shore Drive
It's a short drive

Most people live with a heavy foot on the pedal
But why don't we make the most of the sights?
Pointed to the building I started my business

It went under so I launched a new one two blocks down
Made some change, even made some money
And caught the attention of everyone in town
The dance hall I met the one
Right next to the diner she said yes to seeing me
These landmarks haven't changed over time
And there's the park I finally dropped to one knee

Took me out to cruise down Shore Drive
Look at the school our babies grew up in
They learned to be better than me at everything
There's the train they took when this town wasn't enough for them
There's the store we bought the porch swing
To rest on after decades of building our fortunes
Our favorite restaurant when the little ones visit
And finally home to house we said we'd finally live in

Took me out to cruise down Shore Drive
He said the ride's not over now
The end of the street is where the sand and ocean meet
And there's still some living until you get there somehow
Took me out to cruise down Shore Drive
Said to make the most of the sights
Saw the beauty in broken lights and faded store signs
Make the most of a short drive

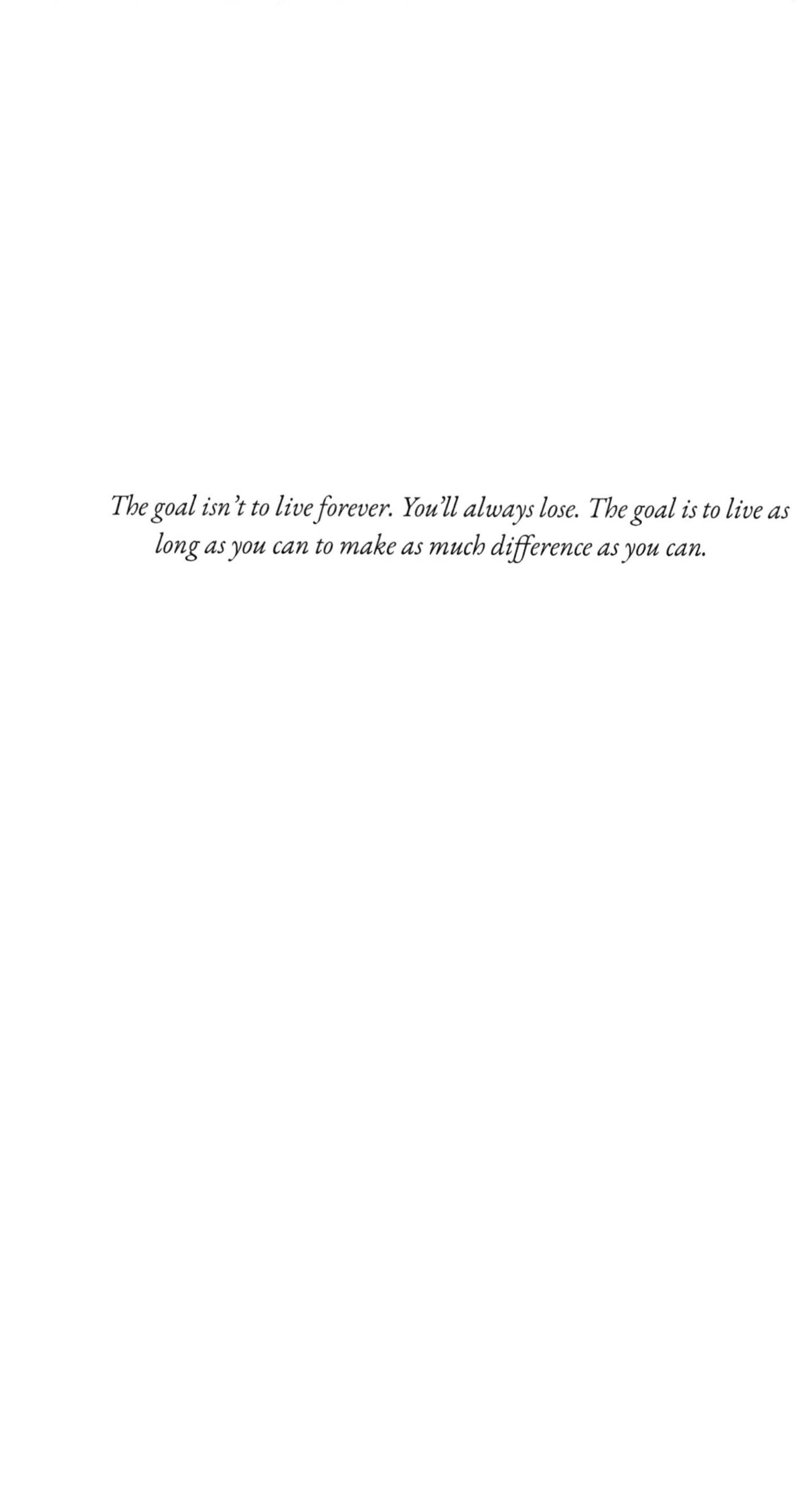

The goal isn't to live forever. You'll always lose. The goal is to live as long as you can to make as much difference as you can.

www.ingramcontent.com/pod-product-compliance
Ingram Content Group UK Ltd.
Pitfield, Milton Keynes, MK11 3LW, UK
UKHW021830270726
14058UKWH00001B/69